Louise Stewart

This is one of a series of books specially prepared for very young children.

The simple text tells the story of each picture and the bright, colourful illustrations will promote lively discussion between child and adult.

First edition

© LADYBIRD BOOKS LTD MCMLXXXIII

Ladybird Toddler Books

puppies and kittens

written by MARY HURT
illustrated by DAVE WESTWOOD
DRURY LANE STUDIOS

Ladybird Books Loughborough

This kitten likes to drink milk.
She uses her little pink tongue.
Do you like milk?

This little kitten is hungry.
He likes to eat fish.
''That tastes good,'' he says.

This kitten has a new toy.
When it is wound-up, the mouse runs
round and round.
The kitten likes to chase it.
He thinks it is a real mouse!

The puppy is having fun
playing with a ball.
The kitten is watching.

These puppies are going to be
good friends.
They have just met.
Look at their wagging tails.
They are happy to see each other.

What has happened to Daddy's slipper?
The puppy has chewed it.
Oh dear! What will Daddy say?

These playful kittens are getting into mischief.
They love to play with wool.
What a mess they're making!

This puppy enjoys a juicy bone.
She can chew it with her sharp teeth.
It is good for her.

This puppy is very thirsty.
He drinks water from
his bowl.

This kitten has her own little door.
She can go out to play
   and she can come in when it rains.

This clever kitten can climb trees.
He has climbed too high.
"Meow," he calls.
Who will help him to get down?

Look at the muddy footprints.
Who has made this mess?
Can you see him hiding?
He knows he has been naughty.

These kittens love to play in a box.
They climb in and then fall out.
They play peepo
and hide and seek.
This is fun!

Are these little kittens going shopping?
I wonder what they would buy?
A juicy fish,
or some creamy milk.

This puppy loves digging holes.
She buries her bone.
She will dig it up later.

This puppy is chasing her tail.
Do you think she will catch it?
Don't get too dizzy!

This little kitten is ready for a game.
She is lying on her back.
She wants to be tickled.
Do you like to be tickled?

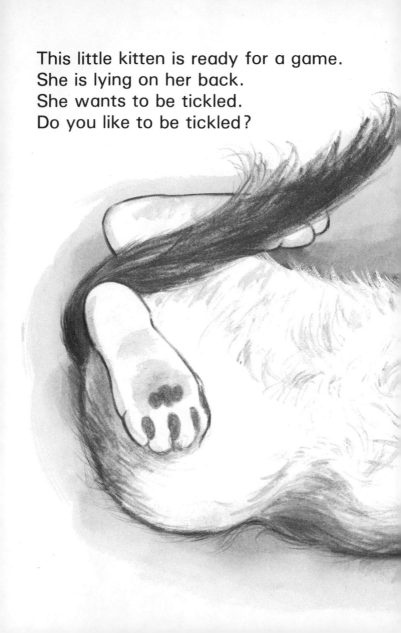

This puppy is on holiday.
He loves to splash in the sea.
When he shakes, water goes
everywhere. Watch out!

This puppy is covered with mud.
She doesn't want a bath.
Look at her trying to hide!

Here are three tired kittens.
They have found a good place
to sleep.
Ssh! Don't wake them up.

This puppy is looking for his dinner.
Is it up here?
Something smells good.
Here it is in his red bowl.

These two friends are sleepy.
They've had a busy day.
Now they are snug and warm.
Goodnight, puppy!
Goodnight, kitten!